THIS CANDLEWICK BOOK BELONGS TO:

_____

_____

_____

_____

First U.S. paperback edition 1994
First published in Great Britain in 1989 by Walker Books Ltd., London.

Library of Congress Cataloging-in-Publication Data

Butterworth, Nick.
My mom is excellent!—1st U.S. paperback ed.
"First published in Great Britain in 1989 by Walker Books Ltd., London"—T.p. verso.
Summary: A young boy describes all the amazing things that his mother can do.
ISBN 1-56402-289-7
[1. Mothers—Fiction.] I. Title.
PZ7.B98225Myj   1994
[E]—dc20   92-43769

4 6 8 10 9 7 5 3

Printed in Hong Kong

The pictures in this book were done in watercolor.

Candlewick Press
2067 Massachusetts Avenue
Cambridge, Massachusetts 02140

MY MOM IS EXCELLENT

Nick Butterworth

CANDLEWICK PRESS
CAMBRIDGE, MASSACHUSETTS

My mom is excellent.

She's a brilliant artist . . .

**and she can balance
on a tightrope . . .**

and she can fix anything . . .

and she tells the most
exciting stories . . .

and she's a fantastic gardener . . .

and she can swim like a fish . . .

and she can do amazing
tricks on a bike . . .

and she can knit anything . . .

and she can tame wild animals . . .

and she throws the best
parties in the world.

It's great to have
a mom like mine.

She's excellent!

NICK BUTTERWORTH was born in 1946 and grew up in a candy shop. He has had a variety of jobs, including working as a typographer, graphic designer, magazine editor, and comic-strip illustrator. He has illustrated a number of books including *Making Faces*, *Busy People*, and *My Dad Is Awesome*. His books *My Grandma Is Wonderful* and *My Grandpa Is Amazing* were both chosen for Fall 1992 Pick of the Lists by **American Bookseller**, which raves, "These two slim volumes are treasures. . . . The texts are simple; the illustrations are colorful, expressive, funny, and warm. [They] will appeal to all ages."